www.trafford.com

North America & international
toll-free: 1 888 232 4444 (USA & Canada)
fax: 812 355 4082

United by Love

A Happy Adopted Child

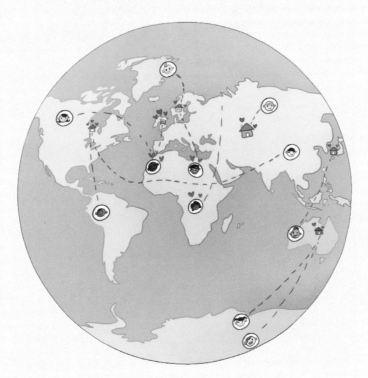

Victoria Rikede

I feel lucky because I was born.

Some families have different skin colors. This is because adoption is done in so many countries around the world. In different continents, you will find people with other skin colors and complexions and cultures.

My parents had to travel to another continent to get me. That is a great miracle. Some parents have not had to travel far away because their children were in the same country as them.

Another way for creating miracles is called surrogate parenting. It means that the children born are actually made by their mom and dad. However, their parents borrow another mother's belly so that their baby can grow safely in them. After the delivery, the baby is then given back to their real parents.

All these families have something in common: love.

My arrival turned out for the best because my biological parents were wise enough to share me with my parents.

Sometimes adoption is done directly from biological parents to new parents, and sometimes the biological parents take their baby to an orphanage, and once there, the child unites with their new parents.

I know that I was wanted because I got the privilege to be loved and to love.

Even though it might look like I was not wanted by my biological parents, I feel they loved me enough to allow my parents to love me. My parents got me because they loved me and wanted me right from the moment they set their eyes on me.

I am indeed a lucky child. I'm grateful for being me. I'm grateful for my parents and the rest of my family. I was born lucky.

Sometimes I think that my friends do not understand me. They feel sorry for me because I'm adopted! What they don't realize is that I'm lucky to be loved by many, and I was wanted by my parents.

One day when they have grown wiser, they will understand that the world has different family structures and the fact that I feel lucky to be a member of my family.

We might not have the same skin color, but we are united by love.

I'm not ashamed to tell the world about my life, and I do not wish my parents to be ashamed either. Our family is blessed, and that is what matters. We stick together because we chose each other.

We are united by love.

Lightning Source UK Ltd.
Milton Keynes UK
UKHW050447300421
382873UK00002B/16